This Little Tiger book belongs to:

Mabli

Zeren

For Maxine and Chris – J C

LITTLE TIGER PRESS LTD,
an imprint of the Little Tiger Group
1 Coda Studios, 189 Munster Road, London SW6 6AW
www.littletiger.co.uk
First published in Great Britain 2012
This edition published 2016
Text and illustrations copyright © Jane Chapman 2012
Visit Jane Chapman at www.ChapmanandWarnes.com
Jane Chapman has asserted her right to be identified
as the author and illustrator of this work under
the Copyright, Designs and Patents Act, 1988
A CIP catalogue record for this book is available
from the British Library
All rights reserved • ISBN 978-1-84869-696-9
Printed in China • LTP/1800/3415/0820
6 8 10 9 7 5

I'M NOT SLEEPY!

Jane Chapman

LITTLE TIGER

LONDON

At bedtime, Grandma always carried Mo up to the top of the tree.

"It's a long way up for a little owlet," she puffed.

Hop... Jump... Flutter...

FLUMP!

"Ooof," she huffed,
sliding him down.
"Here we are!"

Grandma smoothed soft leaves
into a cosy nest, and sat Mo
carefully in the middle.

"Play with me?" giggled Mo.

"No, Sweetie, it's time for bed," smiled Grandma. And she blew him a kiss, and hopped down to her book.

The stars were fading when
Grandma heard a rustle.
"Is that you, Mo?"
"Yes! . . . And I haven't had
my Bedtime Biscuit!"

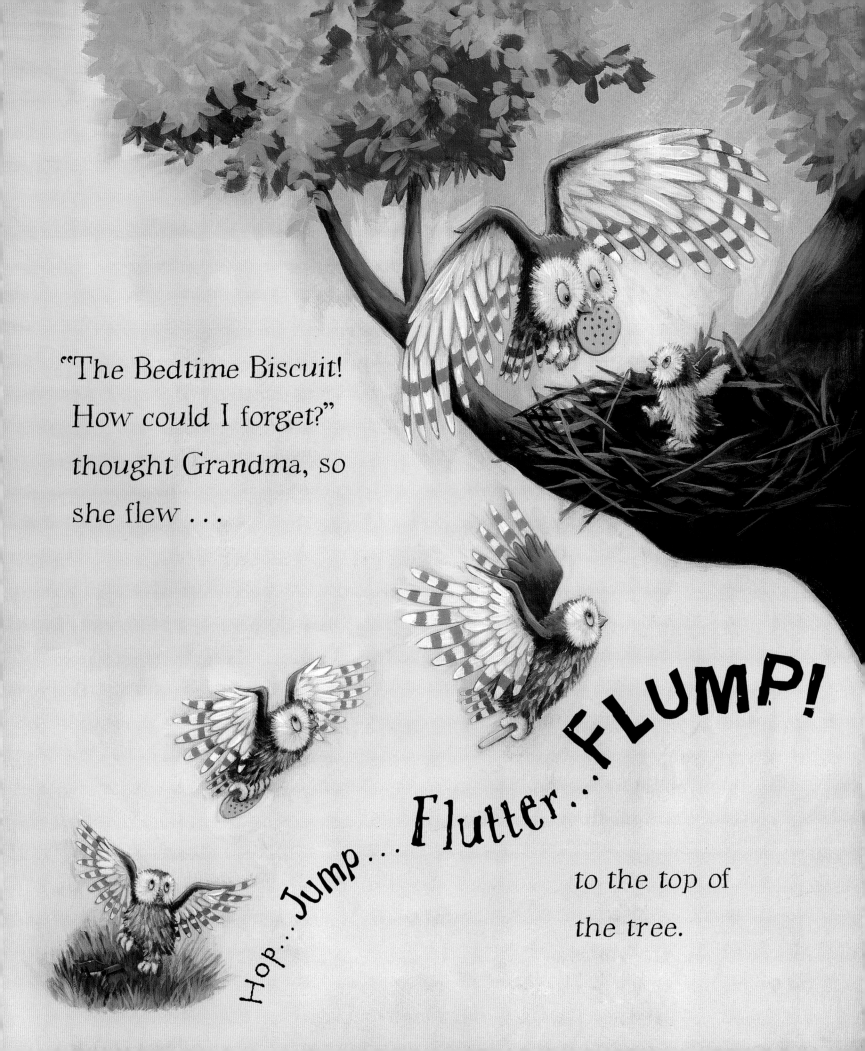

"The Bedtime Biscuit! How could I forget?" thought Grandma, so she flew . . .

Hop . . . Jump . . . Flutter . . . FLUMP!

to the top of the tree.

Grandma sat and waited for the Bedtime Biscuit to be finished.

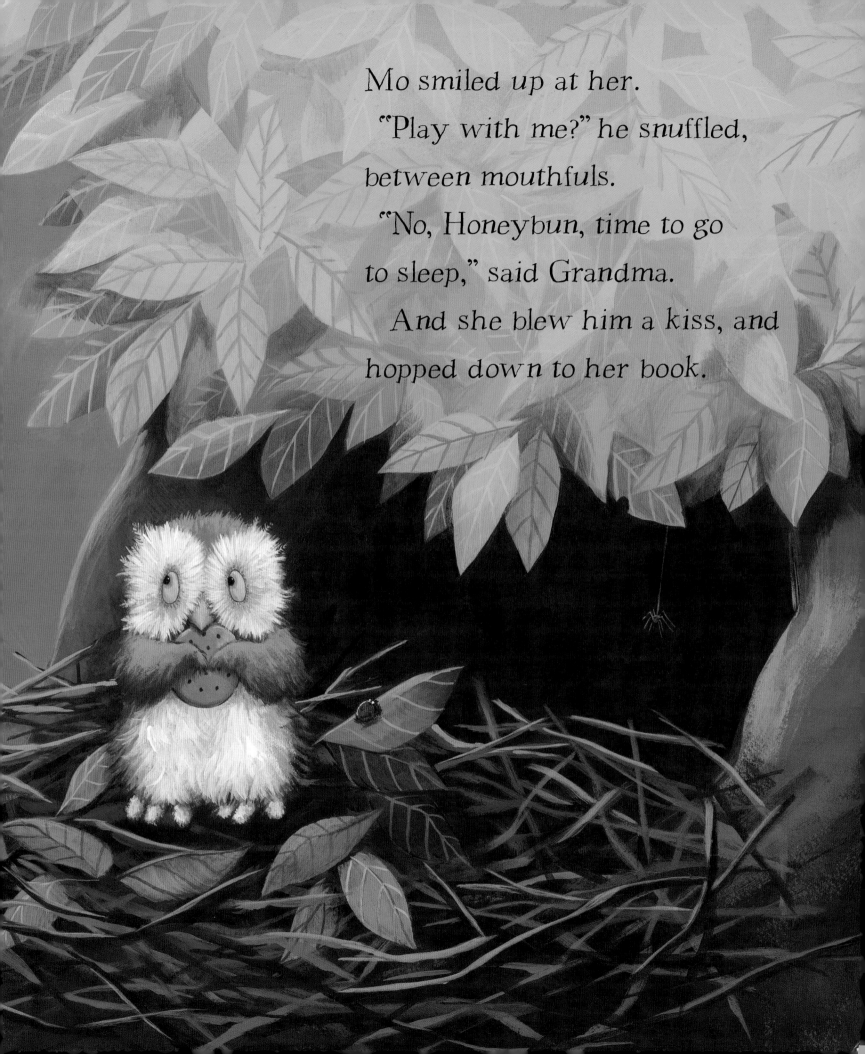

Mo smiled up at her.

"Play with me?" he snuffled,
between mouthfuls.

"No, Honeybun, time to go
to sleep," said Grandma.

And she blew him a kiss, and
hopped down to her book.

The last bats were going home when leaves began to rain down from above.

"Mo," Grandma called, "is everything all right?"

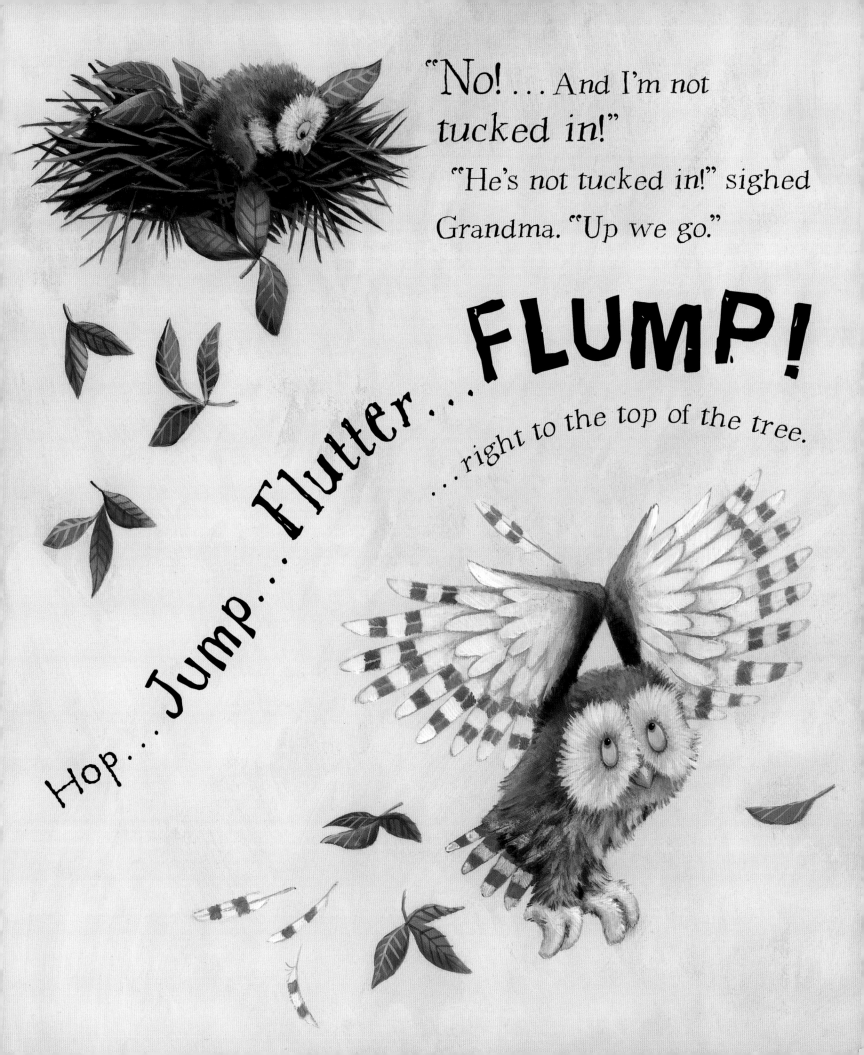

"No! ...And I'm not tucked in!"

"He's not tucked in!" sighed Grandma. "Up we go."

Hop.... Jump.... Flutter.... FLUMP!

...right to the top of the tree.

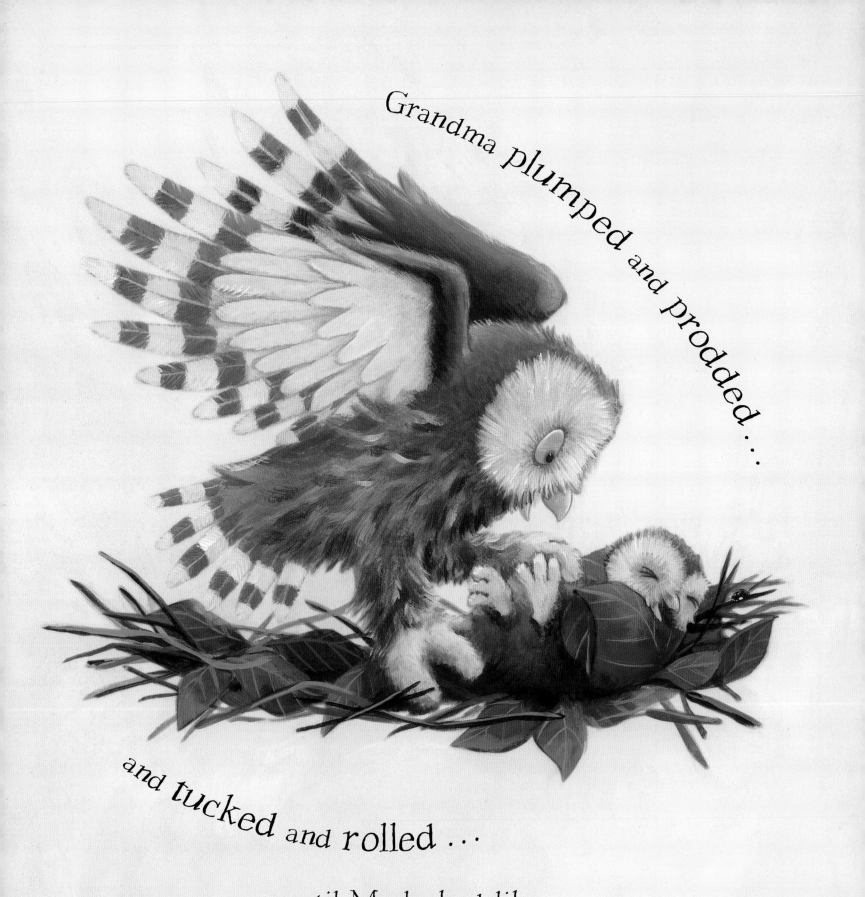

Grandma plumped and prodded...

and tucked and rolled ...

until Mo looked like a
wriggly, green pancake.

"Play with me?" he laughed.
"No, Pickle, it's BEDTIME," said Grandma.
"No more noise now ... unless there's an
Emergency." And she blew him a kiss, and
hopped down to her book.

Grandma sat in the stillness.
All was quiet at last. She was
just about to start reading when . . .

"GRANDMA, GRANDMA!
IT'S AN EMERGENCY!"

"IT'S AN EMERGENCY!"
thought Grandma. "Oh my goodness!"

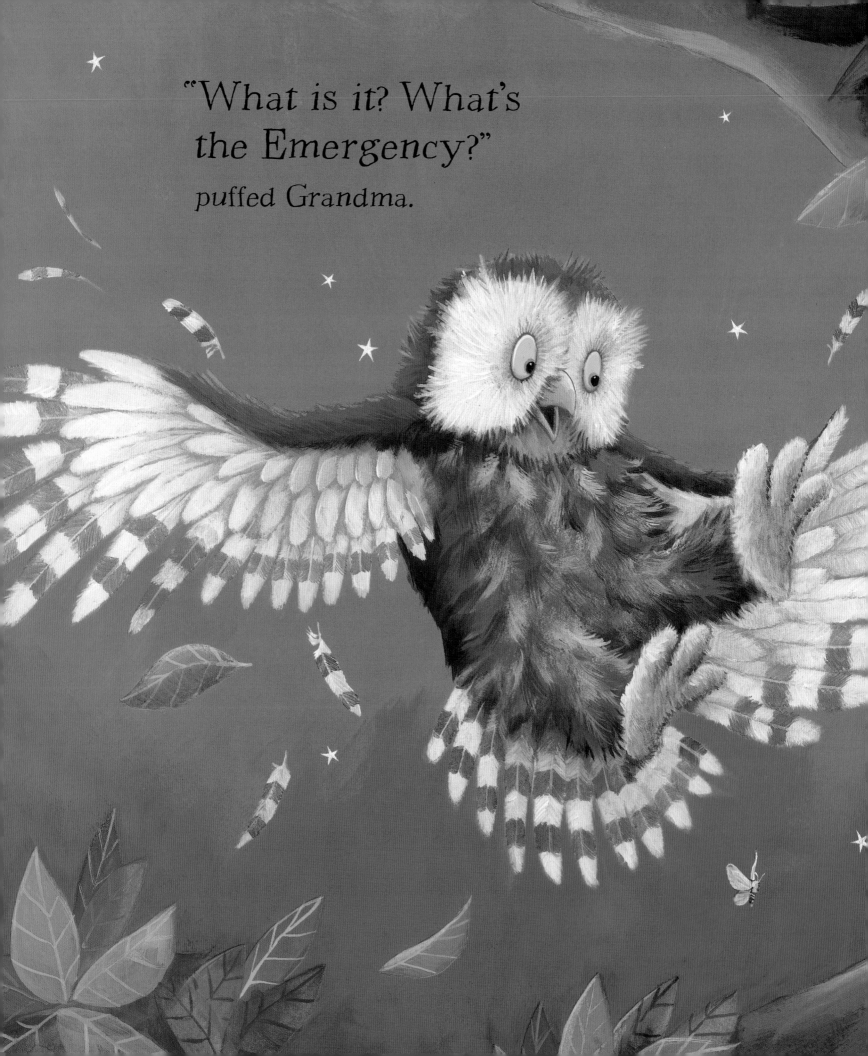

"What is it? What's the Emergency?" puffed Grandma.

"I'm not sleepy!" said Mo.
"I don't want to go to bed.
I want to play!"

Grandma squeezed into Mo's cosy
nest next to him and cuddled him.
"The thing is, Mo, it's bedtime, and at bedtime
SOMEONE has to go to bed," she said.
"So, I have a very good idea. I'LL go
to bed, and YOU can stay up!"

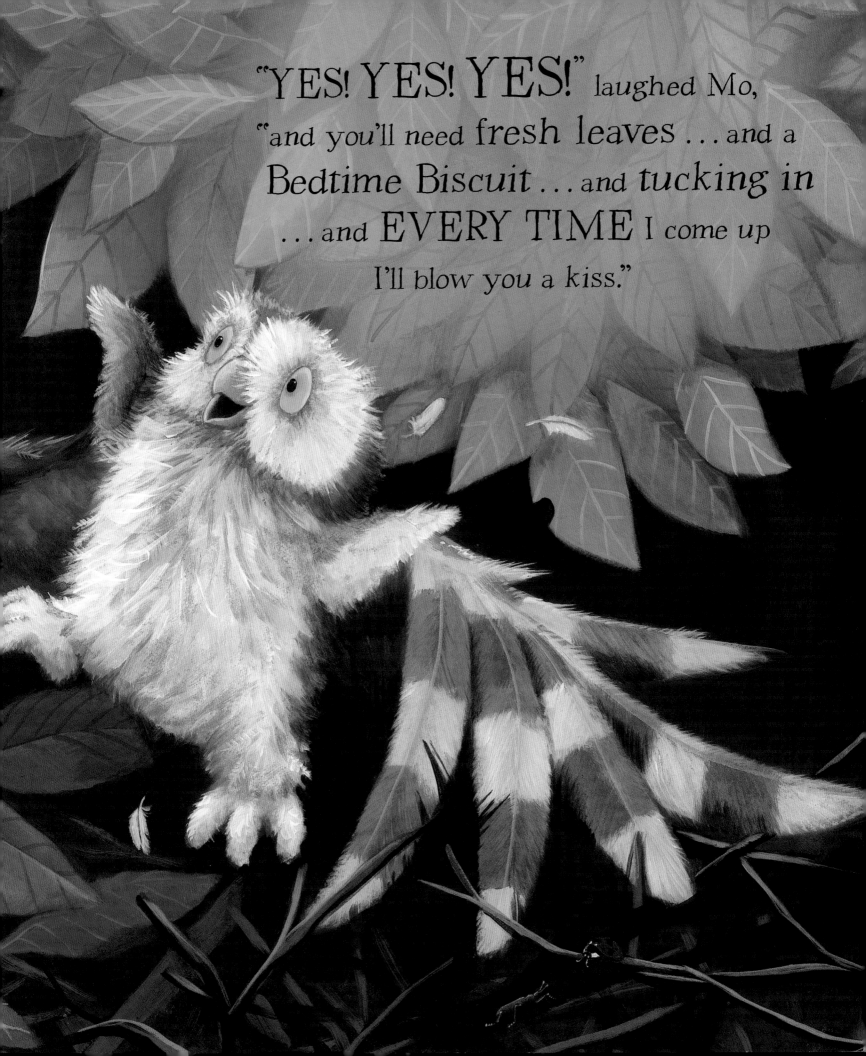

"YES! YES! YES!" laughed Mo,
"and you'll need fresh leaves ... and a
Bedtime Biscuit ... and tucking in
... and EVERY TIME I come up
I'll blow you a kiss."

Mo was very busy.
He didn't have time to play.
It was hard work putting
Grandma to bed.

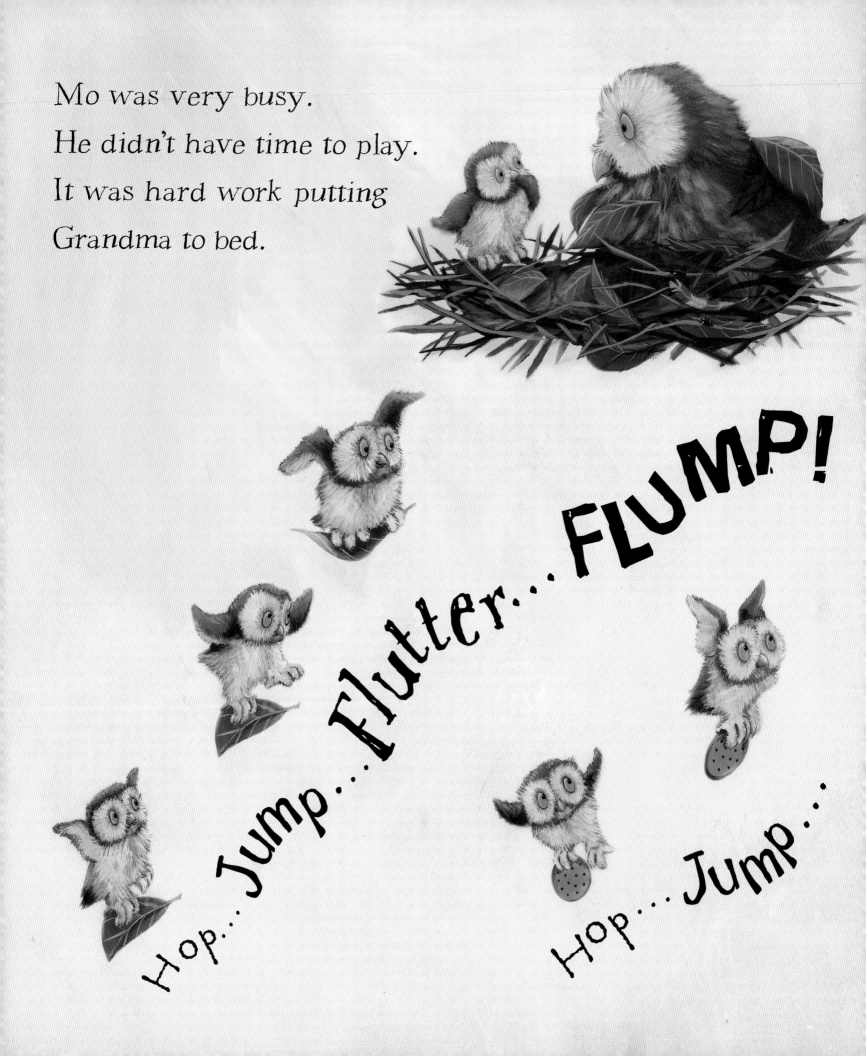

Hop... Jump... Flutter... FLUMP!

Hop... Jump...

Flutter . . . FLUMP!

Flutter . . . FLUMP!

Hop . . . Jump . . . Flutter . . . FLUMP!

Most of the stars were gone when a
little voice called up from below.
"Grandma? . . . I'm really sleepy."
"Of course you are, Poppet, it's very
late!" said Grandma.

And she hopped down the tree to her favourite owlet. "On my back," she said.

Hop...

Jump...

Flutter...

Grandma carried Mo...

all the way up...

to his nest...

FLUMP!

at the top of the tree.

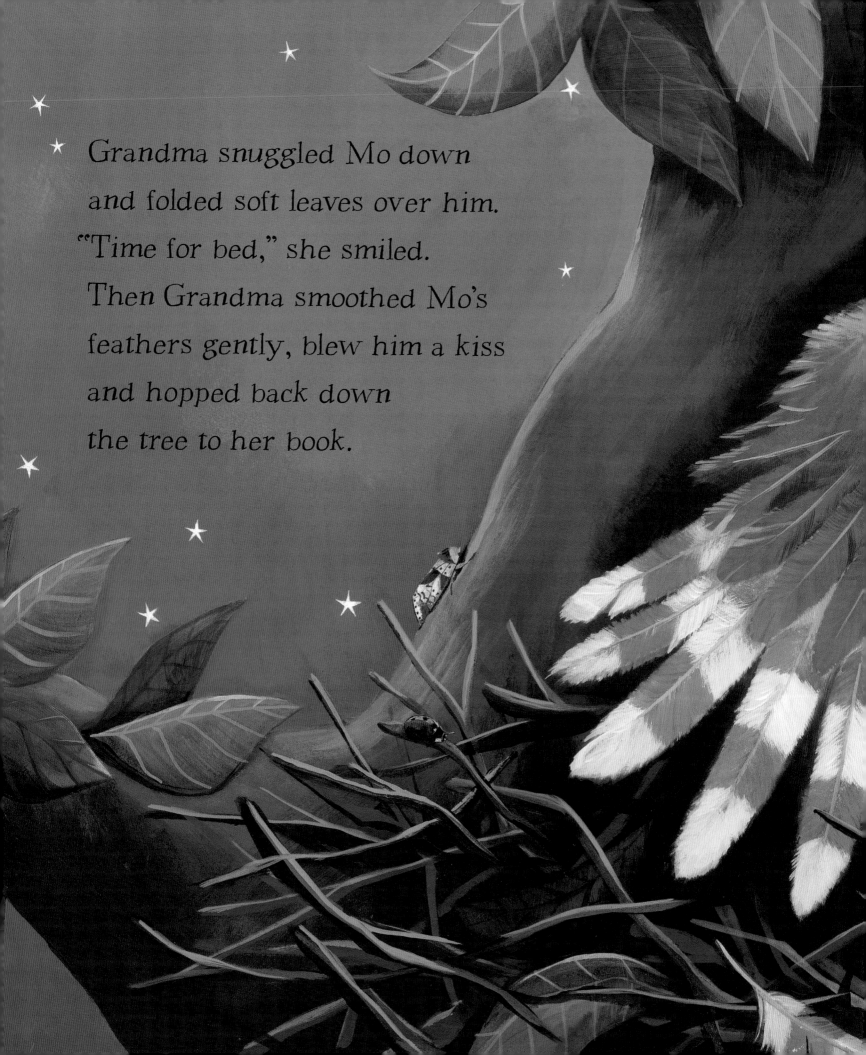

Grandma snuggled Mo down
and folded soft leaves over him.
"Time for bed," she smiled.
Then Grandma smoothed Mo's
feathers gently, blew him a kiss
and hopped back down
the tree to her book.